That Car!

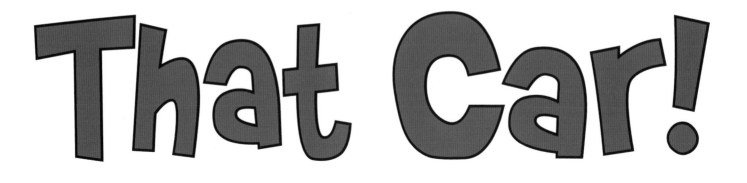

Cate Kennedy

illustrated by Carla Zapel

ALLEN&UNWIN
SYDNEY·MELBOURNE·AUCKLAND·LONDON

For Violet – CZ
For the great kids at Benalla P-12 Primary School – CK

First published in 2014

Allen & Unwin
83 Alexander Street
Crows Nest NSW 2065
Australia
Phone: (61 2) 8425 0100
Email: info@allenandunwin.com
Web: www.allenandunwin.com

A Cataloguing-in-Publication entry is available
from the National Library of Australia
www.trove.nla.gov.au

ISBN 978 1 74331 095 3

Cover and text design by Sandra Nobes and Carla Zapel
Set in 16 pt Whipsmart by Sandra Nobes
This book was printed in January 2014 at Everbest Printing Co Ltd
in 334 Huanshi Road South, Nansha, Guangdong, China.

1 3 5 7 9 10 8 6 4 2

We found the old car in the shed
the very first day we moved to the farm.

An old lady called Mrs Crosbie had owned the farm before us. 'That car's been in our family for sixty years,' she said. 'It doesn't go too far nowadays, though.'

She stood looking out across the paddocks for a long time before her nephew helped her into his shiny new car and drove away.

We asked Dad and he finally pushed the old car out of the shed and under the peppercorn tree. 'I'll take this old clunker down to the scrapyard one day,' he said. 'But you kids might as well play in it for the time being.'

Joey jumped straight into the driver's seat, holding tight to the steering wheel.

'Let's hit the open road!' Luke shouted. 'Where to, Ellie?'

Buckingham Palace was the first place we went to,
far across the sea. That car knew just what to do.

CAR 123

'My goodness, what a splendid vehicle,' said the Queen. Everybody cheered. We made the Queen a cup of tea because queens drink tea all day long.

When we went to Mount Everest, we took it in turns to drive.
We snuggled under the blankets at Base Camp,
telling snow stories and hearing the wind howl.

Mum had to bring provisions out for us.

That car! Our dog Chippy had puppies in it,
right there in the back seat.

All the puppies won ribbons
at Ruff's International Dog
Show, even the naughty
black-and-white one.

BEST IN SHOW

RUFF'S

The stars were out by the time we flew home.

Chippy and the pups were curled up asleep on the leather seat, warm as toast.

Safari! 'Quick, get protection!' yelled Luke.

'It's a rhinocersaurus!'

All kinds of wild animals had come to drink
at the waterhole. 'Lucky we've got the safari-jeep,
that's all I can say,' panted Luke. 'Here, Ellie,
you drive while I take pictures.'

'Look over there, Luke,' I said.
'A rare one-horned buffabulleroo!'

Now for the supersonic jet speed record. 'My turn with the goggles!' I yelled. 'Hey, here comes the jet fuel scientist!'

Mum laughed and took off Joey's hyperblaster helmet. 'So that's where that got to,' she said. 'Kids, we've got a visitor.'

We looked and saw Mrs Crosbie at the back door. 'My goodness,' she called as she came closer. 'Is that the old car?'

Suddenly the car looked different.
Living under the tree had faded its
paint. Chippy's pups had chewed
the armrests. There was still hay in
the back from the time we'd carried
Kryptonite home from the moon,
and Joey's flippers from the Great
Barrier Reef snorkling trip. Maybe the
seawater had caused all that rust.
We thought we were in big trouble.

But Mrs Crosbie just smiled and smiled.

We had afternoon tea and she couldn't stop telling
us stories of the places she'd been to in that car.
We told her everywhere we'd been in it, too.
Mum and Dad couldn't get a word in.

She showed us an old photo of the car when it was
all new and shiny. Sitting inside was a beautiful
smiley bride holding a big bunch of roses.

'You got married in the old car!' I said.
She had exactly the same smile
as the girl in the photo.

Mum stood up. 'Those rosebushes are
all in flower right now, Mrs Crosbie,' she said.
'Come on – let's pick you a bunch.'

After Mrs Crosbie left, we played weddings
under the peppercorn tree. We made a path
of rose petals and Dad got out the camera.
'Say cheese!' he said. 'Get your hat on, Luke.'

'You may now kiss the bride!' Mum announced.
'No way am I kissing Ellie,' shouted Luke.

'All weddings need a chauffeur, of course,'
Dad said, climbing into the driver's seat. He didn't
seem in any hurry to go and feed the cows.

The old car looked great, all happy and
decorated for the wedding. 'We may as well
leave it out here under the tree,' said Dad.
'After all, it's not as if it's going anywhere.'

How could he say that? That car!
That car was going everywhere.